Dedication

This book is dedicated to Ansley Brielle Thomas,
my Sweet and RHOyal daughter

Monk Monk was a monkey who was everyone's friend.

She was a happy hopper whose games never seemed to end.

Monk Monk had big eyes, a long tail, and fur that was brown.

She had a beautiful smile that could turn any frown upside-down!

Monk Monk was adventurous and enjoyed being free.

But she was not your ordinary monkey, you see.

She was often chased by bees when she swung around trees.

Her family would scream, "Monk Monk! Please sit down, geez!"

She was a curious monkey, and that was no doubt.

So, Monk Monk always wanted to figure things out.

Glider the Baboon was Monk Monk's best friend.

He was wiser and older, but Monk Monk was much bolder.

He knew that Monk Monk had a habit of getting into
sticky situations.

From tricks to schemes, she couldn't resist the temptation.

One day, Monk Monk and Glider were playing hide-and-go-seek.

Glider was first to go hide, but silly Monk Monk would always peek!

While hiding in the tree, Glider saw bees swarming around
a pool of bright red water.

"Hey, look over there! Look at the water!" said Glider.

Monk Monk began to jump up and down excitedly.

"I see it, I see it! Let's get closer!" said Monk Monk.

Glider warned, "I don't think that's a good idea, Monk.
Let's play here instead."

Monk Monk asked, "But why is the water red?
I think we should go look ahead."

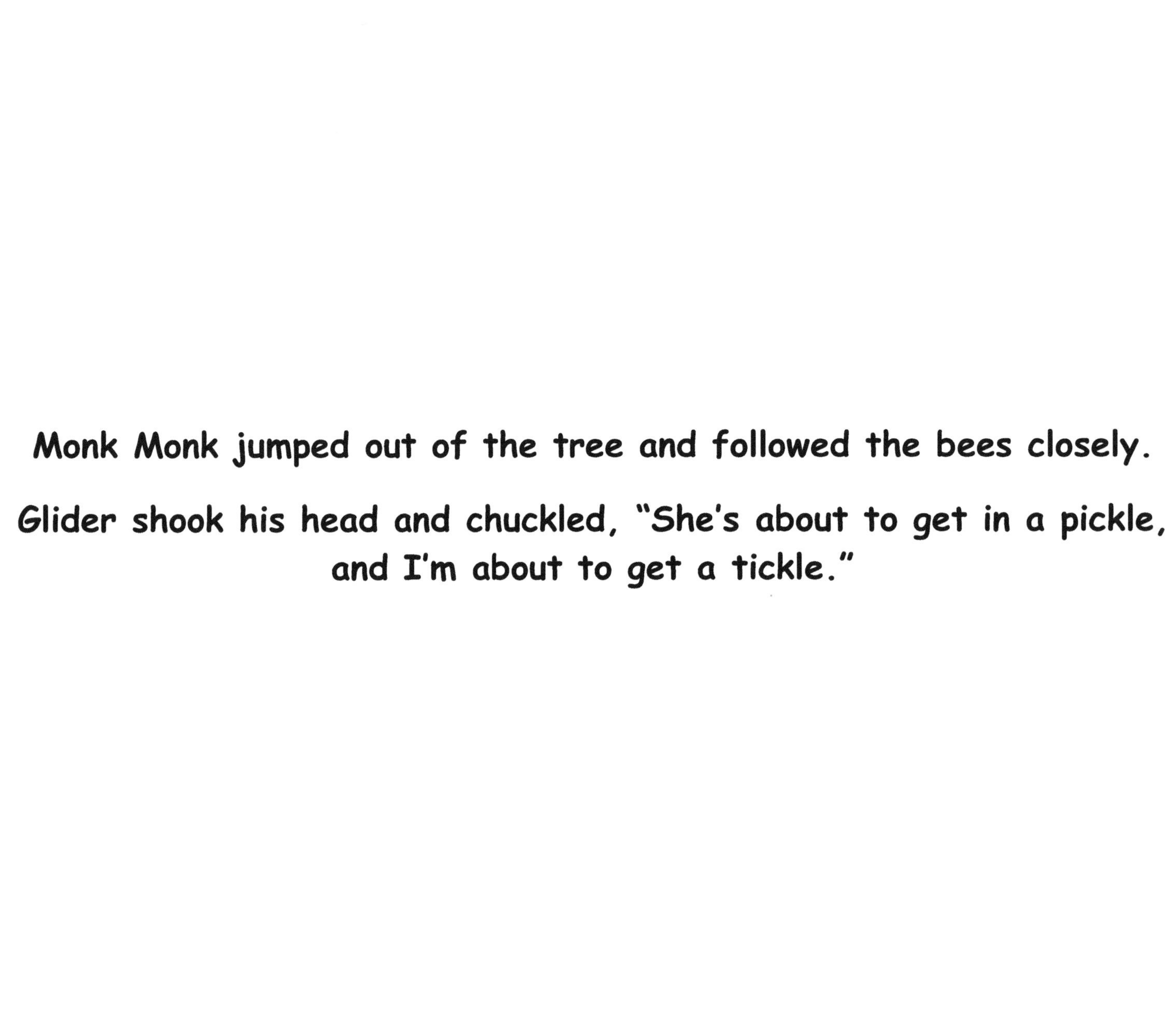

Monk Monk jumped out of the tree and followed the bees closely.

Glider shook his head and chuckled, "She's about to get in a pickle, and I'm about to get a tickle."

Monk Monk saw Mrs. Annie swatting the bees away from her jam.

When Mrs. Annie walked inside the house, Monk Monk crept towards
the bowl like a mouse.

But just as she was about to taste the jam,
she slipped on the floor and went WHAM!

WHAM!

Mrs. Annie came out, saw Monk Monk, and yelled, "SCRAM!"

Monk Monk jumped up and down and ran around like a clown.

But Mrs. Annie had enough and asked, "Will you keep quiet and sit down?"

Monk Monk felt guilty, so she jumped into Mrs. Annie's arms and politely asked, "May I please have a taste? Your jam is the best in town, and I promise not to make a sound!"

Silly Monk Monk's smile always turned Mrs. Annie's frown upside down.

SCRAM!

Monk Monk made it to the water, but to her surprise...

It was a big bowl of strawberry jam before her eyes!

Mrs. Annie was a baker who lived in the woods with her grandcub, and she was making jam for her pies, cakes, and her famous ice cream.

Mrs. Annie was a sweet, old bear who enjoyed helping everyone in the forest. She also had a way of teaching her fellow furry friends a lesson in the fondest way.

This time she made Monk Monk write down one important rule five times for memory:

I will always ask before I touch things that do not belong to me.

Afterward, Mrs. Annie let her have one of her favorite treats: ICE CREAM.

Monk Monk was so excited that she could almost scream!

Mrs. Annie was always so kind to Monk Monk even when she misbehaved, and she realized it was time to apologize for the fuss she had made.

Monk Monk said, "Sorry for trying to eat your jam without your permission, Mrs. Annie!

Mrs. Annie replied sweetly, "I appreciate your apology! Always remember that good manners make a good monkey!"

Mrs. Annie knew that Monk Monk's apology was being sincere and before Monk Monk went home, Mrs. Annie shared one more message:

"Remember, you should always ask before you touch things that don't belong to you. Oh, and you still have my jam all over your shoe!"

QUESTIONS

Who are the characters in the story?

____

____

Where is the setting of the story?

____

____

What is the main idea in the story?

____

____

Do you think Monk Monk made a good choice?

____

____

What do you think Monk Monk learned?

____

____